T0209305

THE PUP OF LUCK

The Adventures of

Leo Pomp

CHERISSE SUDAN

 iUniverse®

THE ADVENTURES OF LEO POMP
THE PUP OF LUCK

iUniverse books may be ordered through booksellers or by contacting:

iUniverse
1663 Liberty Drive
Bloomington, IN 47403
www.iuniverse.com
844-349-9409

Because of the dynamic nature of the Internet, any web addresses or links contained in this book may have changed since publication and may no longer be valid. The views expressed in this work are solely those of the author and do not necessarily reflect the views of the publisher, and the publisher hereby disclaims any responsibility for them.

Any people depicted in stock imagery provided by Getty Images are models, and such images are being used for illustrative purposes only. Certain stock imagery © Getty Images.

ISBN: 978-1-6632-4245-7 (sc)
ISBN: 978-1-6632-4700-1 (hc)
ISBN: 978-1-6632-4037-8 (e)

Library of Congress Control Number: 2022916118

Print information available on the last page.

iUniverse rev. date: 10/17/2022

Acknowledgments

I would like to thank my beloved pet Maltipoo, Leo, for being a wonderful source of creativity and inspiration. I am very grateful to my other dear pets for adding joyous, touching moments to my childhood and life. Most of all, I thank my family, especially my mother, for always motivating me to pursue my dreams, no matter the field.

Chapter 1

Leo Comes Home

My parents brought me home on a quiet, sunlit afternoon. I remember it as if it were yesterday. They drove a light blue car into the garage of their grand house. I remember thinking that I had been dognapped by these tall people.

"Let me out!" I demanded. "Aarroo!" I howled for help. I gnawed at the cage in an attempt to burst free.

A lady with wavy brown hair exited the car. Her husband, who had black hair, came out on the other side. I cowered timidly as my cage was being carried along the path leading to a house. Then, I spotted a curious trio of dogs strolling past the fence, with a dog walker holding their leashes.

"Aarroo!" I yelped. It was the universal cry for help among my kind. Thoughts flew through my mind as to why these dogs were not coming to my assistance. What were they looking at with such curiosity?

I soon discovered that it was me.

Eventually, they became a distant memory, as I went farther into the house with my owners.

"Isn't he adorable, Nathan?" cooed the woman.

The male human chuckled lightly. "He certainly is. We should call him Leo."

"Yes, Leo Pomp," confirmed the female human.

The male lifted me and commented, "I have to say, you were right, Hazel. I didn't think we could handle having another dog, but when I saw Leo, I couldn't help but fall for the little guy."

The woman smiled heartily and said, "The pet store owner said he is very affectionate and loves to play in her garden."

Suddenly, a brown and white bunny with a red collar and long, fuzzy ears appeared from behind the couch, where he had been shyly watching us.

The man rested me on the tiles and said in a gentle voice, "Finnley, meet your new brother, Leo Pomp." The bunny quietly hopped towards me, twitching his tiny nose.

Finnley introduced himself, "Hi, I'm Finn." Physically, he was not much smaller than me and so cute. He said that he had lived here for a year.

I felt like he was the only one who would understand me. My eyes were filled with sorrow. "Where am I?" I asked.

The bunny answered, "You're on Deluxe Street, the fancy pet neighborhood."

I whined, "I miss my sister! I want to go home! Please help me!"

Finnley looked confused. "But this is your new home. Our owners bought you."

"Bought me? I didn't want to be bought. I'm not a toy. I was just taking a long nap with my sister, and the next moment, I was in the blue car. I did not even get a chance to say goodbye. Sure, these humans do not seem like bad people, but they are strangers!" I declared.

The couple heard me whimpering. The lady said sympathetically, "The poor baby must be missing his family. I'm surprised that the owner of the pet store even sold him at two months old."

Her husband nodded, filled a bowl with Puppy Chow, and gave it to me.

Food! That always made everything better. I could never get enough of the delicious smells. But suddenly, my stomach started to ache.

"What's wrong?" Finnley asked.

"My tummy hurts!" I squealed. I lay on the carpet, hoping that it would go away.

Finnley could hear my gurgling stomach. "Wow! Sounds like a tornado!"

I began to howl. Why was this happening? Did they put something in my food? It tasted just like the kind I ate back home. This day was shaping up to be the worst. After being dognapped, I was food poisoned!

The woman heard me whimper in pain, so she patted my head and checked my temperature. She said that I had a fever. She told her husband and called my old family. Then she rested a cool washcloth on my forehead.

With worry, her voice raised as she said, "Leo Pomp hasn't been vaccinated yet. He could have worms, Nathan. The pet shop owner said that we can return him and they will care for him until he's better."

Unsure, he responded, "I don't know. The lady and her kids seemed very attached to Leo. What if she doesn't want to return him after he's better and gives us a refund?"

Surprised, his wife said affectionately, "We're attached to him too."

The husband concluded, "Then I will call our previous vet, and we will handle the problem."

In an hour, the vet arrived and parked her white vehicle at the side of the road by the house. The other dogs in the neighborhood recognized the vehicle and started to bark loudly.

The vet greeted us on the porch. "Thank you so much for arriving on such short notice," said the woman.

"Of course." The vet checked my temperature, weighed me, and listened to my heartbeat and breathing with a silver, shiny piece of metal.

I whined to Finnley, "It's so cold!"

The vet said that I had worms and pulled out a long, thin needle. I started to pant in fright, and Finnley's eyes widened. The brown-haired lady held me and tried to comfort me while the vet swiftly injected me. "Ow!" I yelped, but the vet gave me a bone-shaped biscuit and some weird-tasting medicine.

The vet said to the lady, "Continue monitoring him, but he should be okay by tomorrow." She gave the lady the medicine and advised that I should be vaccinated when I was healthier.

The man patted me and joked, "Wow, you really have work cut out for us, boy."

The lady laughed lightly and turned on the television to relax. I started thinking that maybe this family wasn't so bad after all. At least my tummy wasn't hurting that much anymore, and I felt so grateful. I licked the lady's feet in gratitude, and she cooed at me.

As I rested my head near her feet, she picked me up and cuddled me. I whimpered in relief. This was the only source of comfort I had felt after the horrible ordeal I experienced. I supposed that I could give these two a chance, although I still felt loyalty to my previous family. Perhaps there was more to these people than dognapping.

This was the start of my life with this new family.

Cherisse Sudan

Chapter 2

Leo Makes a Friend

As the weeks went by, I recovered from my illness. I still missed my sister and family, although my new family was so affectionate and had bought me so many toys. I had accepted them as my parents, and I was glad that I did. I realized that it was possible to love another family and still be a loyal dog. You can't limit love.

I was now four months old. I loved to race around in the yard and scatter my toys everywhere, like I was having a treasure hunt.

The clouds parted as the sun smiled widely in the pink-painted sky, shedding all of its warm light onto the streets. I was an early bird and sped through the dog door, eager to start my day, full of enthusiasm. I was slightly taller and longer, and my fur had grown all over my body.

As the sky began to change to blue, I darted toward the white picket fence, barking boisterously at the oncoming mailman.

Finn came out through the dog door and yawned, "Why do you always make so much noise in the morning, Leo?" Finn had grown a bit larger as well. He was now my right-hand man; Finn was the adorable nerd, and I was the strong, brave, winsome canine. I was very protective of Finn.

"I have to alert Momma and Papa to start the day," I told him.

The rabbit quietly retorted, "Why?" as he brushed the fur on his ears with his little paws.

"They have to go to work, Finn."

Then we heard our neighbor yelling at Rocky, his brown Belgian shepherd dog, to stop tugging at the leash and get into the car to head to police training school. Troy, Rocky's owner, thought Rocky was lazy, but Rocky had to work every day and on weekends also. That's why he was always tired and hated school. So, he hid in his yard every morning. He would wake up early and come home late.

I never knew that dogs could have bags under their eyes until I met Rocky. He always whined that he never wanted to be a police dog, but his owner, who worked as a bodyguard, kept forcing him. Rocky wanted to be an actor, but his owner would just complain about his lackluster, indolent personality and wish that he had gotten a German shepherd instead.

Rocky would tell me through the fence to be a good dog so that my parents would not send me to dog training school. He complained that at the school, he was given a bath with cold water, stuffed with dry biscuits, and was not allowed to nap or play. Furthermore, the exercises were rigid and the trainers looked mean. What a nightmare! I detested being forced to do things that I did not want to do, and no one could make me do them. Momma always said I was full of spirit—whatever that meant.

Sometimes, Finn and I played a game of cricket. Finn would push a small ball with his forelegs, and I would bat it with a plastic bottle. I shouted happily, "Ha! Take that!" I loved that game.

I was quite inventive and a little competitive. We never really needed anybody else to play with once we had each other. I did not care to meet new dogs. They would probably try to steal my toys anyway. After our games, Finn and I would run inside to greet Momma and get treats.

One morning while Momma was preparing breakfast, she turned on the television to keep abreast of events taking place. A dog competition was on. The announcer said, "And now, we have our star dog, Rage, the American Akita."

I gave a high-pitched bark of excitement. The camera zoomed in on Rage, a large, muscular, brindled, serious-looking canine. He had a curled tail, strong neck, erect ears, thick muzzle, and the head of a bear. The dog wore a thick chain and a bone pendant.

On hearing the command "Go!" Rage confidently sped through the tunnels and went on the seesaw. The announcer commented, "I tell you, folks, Rage is truly the most driven canine in this new generation of competing dogs. He's good at the agilities, weight-pulling, swimming, hare-coursing, and obedience, and he can rip a disc apart!"

Finn's eyes dilated in fear as he gulped, "*Hare* coursing?"

I shook my head, "He probably catches them, then lets them go."

The commentator continued, "And he's done! That was the shortest time recorded. Great things are expected from Rage in the finals."

I howled in ecstasy. Momma said sharply, "Leo Pomp! Howling is rude!"

Shamefully, I looked down, and Papa begged, "Hazel, he's just a puppy."

Momma continued, "Yes, but if we don't train him, he'll never learn."

Papa patted me on the head, comforting me, and said, "It's okay, pal."

Suddenly, Momma shrieked, "Ow!" She looked down to see Finn nipping on her toenail. He stopped and silently gazed at her, baffled at her loud outburst. Finn was like a cat and dog in one—a ninja creeping up on you before you know it.

Momma went on, "Finnley! If that's your way of telling me that I need a pedicure, message received."

Papa laughed, and I smiled. Finn hopped around and pooped all over the mat. Momma sighed and cleaned it up, then got dressed in gardening clothes to water her plants.

If only the plants were kinder. They often did not live for long, losing water from the sun or being damaged by the harsh, pounding rain. She would become frustrated.

I loved to follow her around in the garden, push my nose in every single plant, lick the leaves, and dig holes. I would sometimes try to hold the watering can for her but accidentally drop it due to its heavy weight. Momma always told Papa to keep me inside while she gardened, but no matter what they tried, they could not keep me from the garden.

As Momma dug a hole for a flower plant, I started to yank some green plants out of the ground. She demanded, "Leo Pomp! Stop biting my plants!"

Momma opened my mouth and realized that the green plants were overgrown weeds. Taken aback, Momma said, "Oh. Sorry, boy." She patted me and continued with her work.

Momma was still gardening when a neighbor stopped by, walking a golden Finnish spitz dog named Dazzling who wore a shiny silver necklace collar with a pendant in the shape of a sun.

Dazzling was wearing a small purple sun visor around her short, pointed ears. She had abundant fur and a curled tail. Why did she need that weird hat? It was not that hot today. She was so fancy and smelt good too.

The neighbor, Paisley, wore a matching visor, a pair of pink-tinted sunglasses, a flowery blouse, and pastel-blue pants. She had blonde curly hair and blue eyes, and she was a lot younger than Momma and Papa. Momma opened the gate for them to come into the front yard and asked, "How's your grandmother, Paisley?"

Paisley sighed, "She can't stop her squabbles with the parrot. As for the monkey, he keeps pulling silly pranks on us. I don't know why she insisted on taking him after she retired."

At that moment, I realized that her grandmother was the retired circus performer known as Grands Pecky, whom everyone thought was bonkers.

Momma gave a small laugh. Yes, even Momma had her own sense of humor. Momma and Papa often complained about Grands Pecky's loud voice.

Paisley continued, "Grands is going down in age, but you know, I admire her a lot. She gave up her magnificent life in the circus and raised Mom really well. I mean, Mom's a big news reporter working abroad! It's just that sometimes, Grands doesn't think things through. It makes me sad. But we love and respect her so much."

Momma cooed, "Aw, yes, she is a remarkable person. She must have done so much in her youth. I bet she is so proud of you and your mother. You speak of your mom's achievements, but you are quite accomplished for your age, and so responsible to be taking care of your grands while your mom finishes up her work contract."

Paisley smiled and said, "Thanks. So, how's business?"

Momma squealed, "Fantastic! Teenagers love sportswear. They wear it to go everywhere now. And your perfume line?"

Paisley replied, "A lot of celebrities want to make their own perfume brands with us."

Paisley finally unleashed Dazzling and took the visor off. "Nice to meet you," Dazzling said to me, waving her golden paw and flashing a smile of pearly white teeth that smelt minty. "What a polite, adorable pair you two are."

"How old is Dazzling now?" asked Momma.

Her friend responded, "Three years. She's doing really well in the obedience trials and dog shows. Do you plan to enroll Leo in anything?"

Momma sighed. "I would like to, but Nathan insists that Leo does not need to work. He spoils that dog so much. Besides, Leo Pomp is a Maltipoo. I believe that competitions in our town only allow purebred dogs, not designer dogs."

Paisley thought about it for a moment and suggested, "Hmm, well, maybe you can start a petition…Oh! You should speak to Miss

Esther about it. It's unfair that mixed breeds can't compete. It's time for that to change. Why must our town be the only one to have this regulation?"

Momma looked thoughtful for a moment and mumbled, "That's not a bad idea..."

Paisley went on, "There are even competitions for bunnies. Finn is one year old now—he would be great at the hopping tournament. Animals need to be stimulated, Hazel, or else they turn that energy into destruction! I mean, just look at my grandma's monkey—he's too idle!"

Momma laughed and then invited Paisley inside the house for a cup of tea, while the three of us remained outside.

I asked Dazzling, "Did you watch the snippet of the semi-finals this morning?"

She excitedly yelped, "I love Sphinx!"

My tail wagged. "I want to be like Rage!"

The same dog walker I saw on the first day of my arrival was out walking with the same three dogs. He stopped in front of our fence for the dogs to take a break.

Malik, the basenji, who had overheard what I was saying, looked over the fence and mocked, "Ha ha! Keep dreaming, toddler!"

Irritated, I replied, "I can be Rage if I want!"

Wayne, the boxer, jeered, "Look at you playing with a stuffed toy and a bunny."

Finn meekly said, "That's not nice."

Malik growled and wickedly smiled, revealing his fangs. "You could easily turn into a plush toy too."

I growled, infuriated. "Leave him alone!" I stood my ground, unafraid, still growling ferociously as a frightened Finn cowered on his hind legs.

Wayne joined in with Malik saying, "Don't mess with us, pup."

Ted, the Saint Bernard, huffed, "Yeah, chump! We're all older than you. I used to work in the navy. You don't want to upset me. You hoodlums today think you're so hip but have no respect. The only chew toys that dogs had back in my day were sticks, and they had great *manners.*"

Malik and Wayne groaned. "We know, Ted. That's all you ever talk about."

Ted huffed and puffed. Then, "A–achoo!" He sneezed all over their faces with his massive snout and great might strong enough to blow the two canines away.

They winced and cried in revulsion, "Ewww, Ted!"

He sniffled, "Sorry! Allergies!"

Wayne mumbled, "Talk about manners."

Ted yelped, "So many flowers and pollen around! Tickled the old snout."

Dazzling walked in front of me and said commandingly, "Enough, you thugs! Have you no pride, threatening a puppy?"

Wayne said with irritation, "Come on, Dazzling. We're just having fun, just like everyone does with your Grands Pecky, heh heh. We're not going to hurt the tyke."

After hearing about how amazing Grands Pecky was from Paisley, I did not find the jokes about her so funny anymore. After all, she was an older person.

The basenji mocked again, "Yeah, he just needs to get realistic dreams. He's no shepherd or retriever. He can't be a hero."

Dazzling remarked sternly, "You shouldn't talk, Malik. Basenjis can't even bark. All you do is yodel like a leprechaun."

Wayne and Ted yelped in astonishment. "Burn!"

Malik cut them off. "Hey! I'm named after a famous singer. Anyway, let's go, dogs!"

With that, they resumed walking in front of the unaware dog walker, who was blasting music in his ears. He quickly held on to their leashes and followed.

I thanked Dazzling.

"Of course!" she replied, "Those ridiculous riffraff will always think they own this street until Sphinx and Rage return."

Chapter 3

Leo Discovers Hero

Curiously, Finn asked, "Do they really live here?"

"Yes!" Dazzling replied. "This neighborhood is for the richest owners and top canines in the Pack Institution. But Rage is the biggest bully here. His gang excludes unpopular dogs, and he detests competition. He only gets along with his brother, Sphinx. Their owners are two brothers: Ivan and Leroy. They are both into monster-truck racing. Sphinx is Ivan's pet and Rage belongs to Leroy."

I was shocked to hear Rage being described in such a manner, but Finn was not.

I responded, "Wow. He sounds awful. Will you introduce me to Sphinx then?"

"I'd love to," she said. "I just have to have my fur groomed, get a pedicure, and have my teeth whitened first. I can't look like a hooligan."

I just looked at her, confused by the meaning of her entire sentence.

"Don't worry, munchkin. You'll find your talent and get your lucky charm."

Still confused, I asked, "What's a lucky charm?"

Dazzling proudly explained, "A tag that pooches get when they find their talent. Mine means that I'm born to be a star."

I asked, "Is that why Malik has music notes on his tag?"

Dazzling answered, "Yes. He yodels for a living. Rage's bone charm means that he's violent at heart, and Sphinx's wings are because he's the most sophisticated, intelligent pooch in the world." Yeesh. She sure was into this celebrity stuff. I never really saw her on television that much, but I did not want to say anything. I only wondered what my charm would be.

We showed Dazzling around the yard. As we neared the old red doghouse at the side of our home, Dazzling asked, "Do you use this doghouse?"

I quickly replied, "No! I live inside the house with Finn and my parents."

Finn said, "It's been here since I first came. I don't know why, but inside is kind of dusty."

The spitz dog gasped. "Oh, darling, don't you know? It belonged to your owners' first dog."

First dog? My eyes widened. Surprised, I asked, "Hey, are you saying that my parents had another dog before me?"

Dazzling nodded solemnly. "I wasn't around when he lived here, but the dogs who were say that your owners had an American foxhound named Hero. He was one of the tallest foxhounds. Hero saved your mother from a bear attack in the woods when there was some neighborhood hike, and they couldn't rush him to the vet in time."

Our jaws dropped, and Finn said, "Wow!"

My eyes widened in disbelief.

Dazzling continued, "They say that your owners took years to move on from his death, but he had lived relatively long for a canine."

I bent my head in sadness, saying in a quiet, hurt tone, "That's why the other dogs said that I was trying to be a hero. I thought that I was the only dog…" I was just a small, fluffy puppy to everybody. Nobody ever took me seriously. And now, I knew why. My parents had a taller, stronger dog before me. How could I ever compare to that?

Cherisse Sudan

Dazzling patted my head, comforting me. "Aw, your family loves you very much, Leo. They love all of you equally. Imagine—he could have been your older brother."

I wondered what that would have been like. Would my parents have even wanted me if they still had Hero? I could only hope so. He sounded like the perfect dog: brave, respected, strong. Now I wanted to do something extraordinary, so I proclaimed, "Well, I want to find something amazing to do to make my parents proud! I want to be like Hero!"

"That's the spirit!" Dazzling cheered.

Finally, Paisley exited the house, bidding Momma goodbye and hooking Dazzling's leash back on. We said, "Thanks for everything!"

Momma returned inside and lay on the couch, reading a book with a picture of a big flower on the cover. Her eyes started to close after a few minutes. Her nap was very short, for I overheard her talking to Papa, saying that she wanted to have a talk with Esther.

"I am going to ask Esther to help me change the regulation that prevents mixed-breed dogs from entering competitions," she said.

Papa responded, "Whoa! Are you ready for all that? Esther is a wonderful lady, but why Esther?"

Momma replied, "Esther has influence. She is the main designer for all of the dog competitions in our town. People rush to her to get their dog costumes made. So, if I can get her to support my petition, that would be great."

Papa added, "Well, maybe that's an idea." He continued, "Dog costumes for competitions are very minimal, but she does spruce up the dogs' appearance and make all of them look like winners. Her secret is her Trinidad Carnival craft."

Momma concluded, "And as for being ready—yes, I am!"

Momma had been up pretty late the night before on her rectangular device that she called 'maptop'. She lay back down to continue her nap, and a quiet snore emitted from her. Gee, she looked tired.

Suddenly, I got an idea to help her get a better nap. I grabbed my stuffed purple teddy and placed it right next to her face on the couch. Momma could use it as a pillow, like I did sometimes. It was my favorite toy and very comfortable. I enjoyed running around with it, biting its ears, and throwing it up in the air. It had my scent and slobber on it if she felt lonely and missed me.

A short while after, Momma awoke, and as she turned, she was faced with the toy's gigantic eyes and big smile. She gasped in surprise, "Ahh! Oh...Leo! Why did you put your chew toy by my face!" Her eyes squinted, and her face wrinkled in discomfort. She moved toward the sink to wash her face, and then she threw my toy in the washer.

In confusion, I tilted my head and made a soft whine. What was she bickering about? I was trying to be nice. Sheesh. Papa would have been more grateful for such a cute teddy.

Sometimes, I would try to follow Momma to the washroom to dutifully guard her, but she always shut me out for some reason. There was a mysterious, oval bowl with water. I tried to reach for a sip of water a few times but I could not reach. I wonder; was she trying to hide it from me?

Momma would usually shriek, "Leo Pomp! Privacy! Give me some privacy, please." She always complained to Papa about my following her foot to foot, but he thought it was adorable.

After Momma was dressed, she cautioned me, "Behave, Leo! I have to meet your father at work. Don't ruin my plants, else it's obedience school."

I groaned. She closed the gate and left. Finn asked, "Why do you go in her garden?"

"I just can't watch the plants die. Plus, she'll be so happy when she sees them blooming."

The rabbit said carefully, "If you break a pot, she'll get mad. You could get sent away to a mean dog training school like Rocky did. Hope you like bathing every day."

I hated baths. They made me feel tiny, wet, and vulnerable. Why were baths even important? I liked smelling like the garden, all covered up in the scent of dirt. It felt natural.

I shuddered and brushed the thought off. "I'll deal with the consequence. Psh, I'm not scared."

Finn added, "For now."

Momma should be grateful for this, I thought. I gingerly pulled and pushed each pot and rearranged them so that the short, smaller ones that were under a big shady tree were now positioned to get sufficient sunlight.

I placed some plants under a draining system at the side of the house. The bunny wondered, "How do you know which plants need more sunlight?"

I answered, "I smell them. You can tell which plants keep moisture."

Afterward, I urinated on the porch mat to show my good manners and because Momma's scent was lingering around and I missed her dearly. I was a good dog; I did not dirty the long tray with the paper so that Momma would not have to clean it.

It felt like years since I had last seen her. I wondered when Papa and Momma would be back from their long journeys.

Finn had his own way of missing our parents. He would nibble Momma's shoes and extension cords and pee on their mat. I had stopped chewing shoes a long time ago because I was a big boy, although chewing rubber did sound good at the moment. We took naps until our parents returned.

After they greeted us, Momma inspected her plants for damages. She said, "That's weird. I thought I had put this potted fuchsia baby plant to the front to get sun."

Papa suggested, "You probably forgot that you moved them."

When Momma got to the door, she shrieked, "Leo Pomp! You used the mat as your pad! Aaah! Leo, you make it hard to potty train you."

Papa rolled his eyes at her dramatic meltdown and cleaned it up. What was she always so furious about? It was like nothing I did was right.

I always brought all sorts of things to her: pine cones to play with, my squeaky bone, plastic bottles, but she always seemed so unappreciative. Now, I jumped on her as she sat on the couch and started to lick her and her hair. It tasted nice—so soft and smooth—and smelled fruity.

She cried, "Oh, Leo Pomp! Fine! I'm not mad; now stop licking my hair."

Papa chuckled, "He's giving you a new hairstyle."

Saliva was the best gel to tame her long, windswept hair. Finn mostly tried to groom our parents' skin. We both agreed that our human parents needed help in staying clean.

Papa did not have as much hair for me to groom. He knew how to take care of himself more than Momma. I love grooming Momma and helping her care for her plants.

It was not long before Momma exclaimed, "Nathan, look! My nasturtiums have grown so quickly, in such a few days! I can now transplant them into the ground."

I smiled at a speechless Finn. I knew the nasturtium liked sun. After that, I decided to continue shifting the flowerpots around for Momma. She usually noticed a change, but Papa often convinced her that she was simply losing track.

Within a month or so, their friends began to compliment Momma about her garden. They said things like, "The flowers are so rich in color! How did you make them blossom so well? Can I take a picture? I want to show my gardener." Momma beamed with pride. Was I not the best?

Eventually, I started to store my own gardening things in the red doghouse, with the help of Finn. To add variety to Momma's garden, I dug holes in the dirt, each the same size. I carefully spilt a pack of flower seeds, which Momma kept on her gardening table, and sprinkled them into the holes. Then I covered them back up. I would take a plastic bottle of water from the case in the storeroom, carry it in my mouth, and water the plants.

Finn spent nights looking at Momma's picture book for ways to improve a garden. He suggested that we use the book to follow as a guide to make compost for the plants. I spent time gathering discarded vegetables, old paper, and shrubs in Hero's doghouse to create compost to nourish the plants. Finn and I also tried to create small mud puddles to attract butterflies, since they need to drink water after having the sweet pollen. More butterflies meant more pollination and more flowers.

Chapter 4

Leo Dances

When Momma arrived home, she moved around the house with great haste, so much so that she forgot to greet Finn and me. *Honk! Honk!* A loud car horn blew in front of the house. It was Paisley and Dazzling.

Momma grabbed me up and shouted to Papa, "Take care of Finn while I'm off with Paisley, Nathan!" She then got into Paisley's vehicle with me.

Paisley assured Momma, "Everything is set!" Inside the car, I greeted Dazzling and Paisley with a lick. I was then overcome by the smell of my favorite not-to-eat food, lasagna.

Once, when I was hiding under the dining table, Papa had fed me a mouthful of lasagna. Momma had been furious, but I remembered the taste. I asked Dazzling, "Where are we going and where is the food?" She seemed just as unaware of what was taking place as I was.

Paisley drove onto the next street and stopped in front of a house. The house belonged to none other than Miss Esther, the fancy designer and influencer.

I whispered to Dazzling that I remembered Momma telling Papa something about Miss Esther and competition.

Miss Esther came out to welcome us and invite us into her home, which was filled with a delicious aroma. The smell was new to my sniffer and sent me wild with excitement.

Momma announced, "We brought lasagna, since we know you probably just got back from work."

I really did not know what Momma was talking about. I did not know anything about Miss Esther and her work.

Miss Esther gushed while holding the lasagna, "How thoughtful of you, but I have a little snack prepared for you ladies. Here, I have it set out. It is bake and shark."

Momma smiled and said, "It looks delicious. Is it a Trinidadian dish?"

Miss Esther replied, "Yes, it is. Now, help yourselves."

My nose was going wild, and my mouth kept watering for the bake and shark.

Momma took a bite and lit up with delight. "Oh, Esther! This is divine! Mmm!"

Paisley chimed in. "I love the sauce. What is it?"

Miss Esther answered, "Tamarind sauce."

While Momma and Paisley ate, Miss Esther gave us doggie treats and patted us. Then she asked, "So ladies, what do you all want to discuss?"

Momma quickly stated, "I am going to petition for the regulation preventing mixed-breed dogs from participating in competitions to be removed in our town, and I need your support since you have great influence."

Paisley further explained, "There are many dogs with special talents that may defy their breeds, so why limit them? Leo is a perfect example. He is a mixed toy dog, but he is super-fast."

Miss Esther looked at me and then Momma. She whispered in a sympathetic voice, "Hazel, you know that it is not the same."

Momma looked teary-eyed. I liked Miss Esther, but I did not like her making my momma teary-eyed. She rarely ever looked like that.

Luckily, Momma sat upright and firmly said, "No, it is not that. I know that they are different. Still, Leo has speed and deserves a chance to compete in competitions suited for his ability. It is the same for all dogs that participate in competitions for which they have a particular ability."

I wondered, *Were they referring to Hero?* They must have been. Momma must have loved him very much. I started to feel a bit sad too. I loved Momma a lot, and I wished that I could take her pain away. Yet, I would never be able to compare to Hero. I was not trying to, but that was all everyone ever seemed to talk about—like I was just a cute distraction, a pipsqueak who knew nothing about the world.

My ears drooped, and I bent my head in despair. Dazzling gently nudged me and cooed in assurance, "Don't worry about it, sweetheart." Still, it felt good to hear my Momma stand up for me.

Miss Esther looked back at us and noticed that Dazzling and I were getting restless. She said, "Okay, Hazel. Let me put my two furry guests out to play." She called out, "Calypso!"

From upstairs came sprinting a jolly white border collie with pointed ears and large patches of dark and light brown fur all over his ears, forehead, and eyelids. His coat was so silky and smooth. He wore a snapback hat backward, a silver chain, and a light blue shirt patterned with palm trees.

I had never seen any dog ooze such coolness. No other pooch ever dressed like him. He was unique—he definitely looked like a star boy. He even smelt cool, like one of those colognes for dogs.

Miss Esther slid the glass door open and put the three of us in the backyard to play. The back of the house was relaxing. Calypso knew Dazzling and invited her to sit on his hammock. He smiled and asked me, "What sports do you like?"

I stated, "I am not sure yet."

Dazzling added, "He likes gardening."

Calypso smiled and joked, "Oh my! I knew a dog back in Trinidad who claimed to be a farmer because he had lived on a cocoa estate. His owner built a barrier to keep him away from the cocoa plantation, since cocoa and chocolate are not healthy for dogs. By the way, Trinidad sells amazing cocoa all over the world to make chocolate. Are you even *allowed* in the garden?"

Dazzling barked defensively, "Oh, of course he is! Leo is the real deal, I tell you."

Taken aback, Calypso backed away from her a bit, chuckling, "Okay, okay. I believe you."

I asked, "Where is Trinidad?"

Dazzling responded, "It is in the Caribbean. Calypso is a Caribbean boy and a great surfer."

I was so intrigued. I yelped, "Really?"

Calypso laughed. "Yes, I used to surf at Maracas Bay. It is a popular beach back in Trinidad."

Suddenly, my eyes caught a strange-looking box. Curiously, I questioned, "What is this?"

Calypso boasted ever so coolly, "Watch and listen."

He pressed the box, and music flew out. Calypso chuckled as I stepped back with a startled response, and he pulled Dazzling out of the hammock to dance. Her eyes widened in surprise as she nervously backed away.

"Oh no, I'm quite all right!" Calypso sang, "Come on, Dazz! Dancing is fun! You just have to feel the beat and get the rhythm!"

She yelped, "I'm not much of a dancer." But every time she tried to leave, he would block her. It was funny.

I was a bit shaky at first, but I started to get the rhythm and danced on my hind legs while lifting my front paws.

Calypso was shaking his tail to the beat of the music, and we all laughed. I had never really seen a dog dance before, and not like this. I started to shake mine as well, and we all howled, "Aroo!"

Calypso grabbed a pair of wooden ball-shaped sticks that were in the hammock and gave me one. He shook his in his mouth, making it release a rattling sound. He stated, "These are chac-chacs—my favorite instruments." It was enjoyable to shake.

Suddenly, Calypso vanished and reappeared with a long stick. He placed each end of the stick on a chair. Then he limboed under it and shouted, "Dazzling! Your turn!"

Dazzling looked so hilarious trying to dance her way under the stick.

Then, Calypso cheered me on. "Leo! Let's see you!"

I shimmied myself under the stick to the beat of the music.

We all howled in delight. I asked Calypso if he was training for the corgi limboing that I had seen on television.

Dazzling and Calypso laughed so loudly that I started to laugh too.

Dazzling said, "This beach boy is not a corgi. He is a border collie."

I asked, "So how come he limbos so well?"

She replied, "Limbo dancing is part of his Trinidadian culture, so it comes naturally to him, I guess."

Calypso nudged me with his nose and joked, "I feel that this boss man is ah Trini. You should visit Trinidad one day with me."

I squealed in elation, "I would love that!" Calypso was so much fun.

Then he stated, "You know what? You can keep the chac-chac—a token from your best Caribbean pal."

Touched, I squealed, "Really?"

He gave a big nod and winked, replying, "You bet, boss man."

Chapter 5

Leo Has a Playdate

A week later, we had a playdate with Dazzling at her house. Grands Pecky was in the backyard, busy on the phone. She shouted, "Fanny! Stop repeating what I say!"

Fanny, the parrot, repeated, "Stop repeating what I say!"

Grands Pecky yelled back vigorously, "I will feed you to Dazzling!"

Fanny squawked, "What?"

Agitated, Paisley turned the television on to tune them out. Another competition was aired. A grey, thin Bedlington terrier, with curly fur and hanging ears, was dancing with a hula hoop, making the crowd go wild.

Dazzling rolled her eyes. "Ugh, I don't see why everyone likes Merle so much. She looks like a granny sheep. I tell you: society has no taste. They prefer grey, shaven sheep like that to pure gold. After her rocky relationship with Wade, the Airedale terrier, she's seeking to pursue someone more popular like Sphinx. It gets on my nerves."

The phone rang. Dazzling listened intently to Paisley's conversation with her golden, pointed ears and gasped with concern, "Oh no!"

"What's wrong?" Finn asked.

"Your father has been injured. He sprained his ankle. Your mother's taking him to the doctor, so you're staying here for the night."

I cried, "What? Taking him to the doctor? That cannot be good! I hope he's okay. He's the best papa in the world!"

What did *sprain* even mean? Humans used too many weird, big words for no reason. I just hated the thought of my family being in pain.

Dazzling said, "I'm sure he will be fine. In the meantime, you two can sleep on my spare bed."

We all went outside in the front. I noticed a daffodil plant in the garden that Momma had given Paisley.

"Oh no! I can't check on the plants!"

Finn assured me, "It's just one night. Momma will still water them."

I noticed a yellow flower that looked dry on Paisley's porch. "You should put this guy behind the other plants to get more shade and water him."

"How do you know so much about gardening?" Dazzling inquired.

"He's always rearranging our potted plants too and doesn't get caught," answered Finn.

"So, Leo, do you know any tricks?" Dazzling asked.

Finn complained, "He jumps around like a pony for food and spins."

Dazzling exclaimed, "Leo! Do you know how long it takes for most dogs to learn that?" She turned to Finn, making him slightly nervous, and said, "Do you jump high too? There are many agility competitions for bunnies. You both are so talented…Why don't you allow me to mentor you?"

We both looked confusedly at each other. I answered, "Sure."

Finn replied, "I have stage fright."

Cherisse Sudan

"We'll work on it," Dazzling exclaimed. "Helping the younger generation find their place would look good on my résumé."

She smiled widely as we watched her, baffled. What was she talking about?

"Leo," she began, "I think that we should begin training you for talent and discipline competitions."

I whined, "I want to do agility too!"

Sweetly, Dazzling explained, "I'm afraid that you may not be able to enter that. They set the obstacles for bigger dogs, more purebred dogs. For bunnies, the courses are made more practical, to suit any size of bunny. Hmm. Let me think. Frisbee! Frisbee competitions can work for any dog and smaller breeds are better at canine freestyle. They look adorable when dancing."

I muttered, "I don't just want to be cute."

Then Fanny flew to the front of us and squawked, "Cute!"

Gino, the monkey, followed and let out a naughty laugh. "Heeheehee whooo!"

I thought, *This monkey has a diaper on and wants to laugh at me. The audacity.* I shouted, "Stop laughing!"

Fanny mocked, "Ruff ruff!"

Dazzling warned, "Be careful. Sometimes Gino takes his diaper off and throws it at you."

Finn twitched in disgust. "What?"

Dazzling shuddered. "And he stole my shampoo and conditioner. It was my worst trip to the spa."

Yikes. Still, I was tired of being called cute and everyone laughing at me. I could do much more than look like a toy. I was not a puppy anymore. I just wanted to show the other dogs that I was a full of ambition.

When we were back inside, Paisley told Grands Pecky, "I'll be back shortly. I'm going to the grocery store so I can make soup for Hazel and Nathan. Watch the pets please." She patted Dazzling on her head and exited the house.

Grands Pecky sat on her rocking chair, and it did not take long for her to fall into a deep slumber, full of snoring. Gino leaped onto her shoulder and untied her hair, searching through it thoroughly for lice.

Then, as the television showed a Jack Russell terrier dancing, standing on his hind legs and flipping through hula hoops, I commented, "Wow, he's a good dancer!"

Dazzling's eyes popped as she got an idea. "You should get into the dog dancing club. Then you'll be invited to award shows and dinners. When you receive your award, thank me in your speech."

After another competition aired, footage was played, showing a tall, lean dog with a black saddle, tan fur covering his limbs, and white tips on his paws and tail. The dog was an American foxhound.

Surprised, Dazzling blurted out, "It's Hero at the agility trials. Looks like a replay."

He did look heroic, warm, and brave in a sort of traditional fashion. The time buzzer went off, and Hero leaped over the hurdles with ease.

I remarked, "He's amazing."

Suddenly, a young Akita dog came out of nowhere and ran beside him.

The judges and the Akita's owner tried to catch him, but he kept escaping their grasp. The crowd started to boo at the younger dog, who ran like he was mad.

In shock, Dazzling gasped, "That is Rage. Hero was startled by Rage, but kept going. Arrogantly, Rage was trying to upstage Hero by trying to outrun him. At least, that was how it looked." She added, "He looks so young and insane."

Rage could not keep up with Hero's speed and Hero still won, despite the distraction. Rage was taken away by his owner, as spectators yelled, "Train your dog!" His face showed shame.

Dazzling stated, "From what I heard, Rage was always jealous of Hero. He hates when other dogs get attention."

I shrieked, "That's terrible!"

She continued, "Never let power get to your head. Now, let's practise. We can reach places, my darlings."

I agreed, "Okay." And with that, we began.

I practised standing on my hind legs, begging, limboing, and spinning. Then, Dazzling and I set up a little obstacle course for Finn. We found long sticks and lodged them in plant pots, and arranged stones for him to hop over. He also practised bouncing off the walls.

"We can meet every day before lunch to practise. One day, I'll visit with Paisley on a walk and you can do the tricks in front of your...um...mother and Paisley so that they can see your talent. Knowing Paisley, she will persuade your momma to enroll you two in competitions in no time."

Finally, Paisley returned from the grocery store. She saw Grands Pecky on the rocking chair. Then, gasping, Paisley shrieked, "Grandma! What happened?"

Snorting for air, the frail lady awakened and mumbled, "W–what?"

Her granddaughter cried, "There is some blue liquid all over the carpet! Oh my goodness! Your hair is blue!"

Grands Pecky's eyes widened as she awoke from her nap. She got up, sped to her mirror, and screamed in shock, "Aaahhh!"

Then we heard the monkey screeching in delight. Our heads turned to Gino, who was jumping up and down, with a bottle of blue hair dye in his hand.

Angrily, Grands Pecky bawled, "Gino! You wicked oaf! You opened my gift pack of dyes! I keep saying that you will raise my blood pressure! Although...the color kind of adds a youthful glow to my face..."

Paisley fretted, "This was an expensive carpet, Grands. It will cost a fortune to clean. I keep telling you to put Gino in his cage. Oh, and you look outrageous."

Fanny flew over to Paisley and repeated, "*Squawk*. Outrageous!" Gino tried to pluck Fanny's feathers. "*Rawk*. Help!" crowed Fanny.

Paisley snatched the bottle of dye from Gino and placed him in his cage, causing him to pout. Then she told Grands Pecky, "You *must* stay indoors for a while. I will dye your hair brown in a few days when the blue starts to fade."

Grands Pecky whined, "But you promised to take us to the park. Gino needs his exercise. That's why he's acting up and I need to walk to keep my blood pressure down."

Paisley sighed and placed a gigantic, flamboyant, floppy hat on her grandmother's head. "Hop in the car. Let's go before it gets late."

I laughed in my mind. This family surely was a circus parade, as Momma would say. So much fun!

The park had such soft, green grass. Finn looked around, commenting, "Wow. There're so many animals."

Dazzling shrugged, "This park is overrated. Other neighborhoods have fancier parks with pools, ball pits, and courses. We could use an upgrade." Sheesh, Dazzling was fussy.

Chapter 6

Leo Meets New Dogs in the Park

I spotted a taunting squirrel and was about to chase it up a tree, but Dazzling picked up on my impulse and uttered without looking at me, "Show dogs don't *chase* animals."

"Oh!" I exclaimed as I froze in my position. The air was fresh and the smell of nature was all around. Everyone was in a relaxed mood.

Grands Pecky allowed Gino to scamper freely, while Paisley spoke to a friend on a distant bench.

I commented, "This tree is so big! No wonder squirrels love it."

Dazzling replied, "The dogs call it the 'Tree of Bark.' It was planted here many years ago by someone unknown. All dogs leave their mark on it by scratching it with their claws."

Suddenly, all the dogs ceased what they were doing. They turned toward the entrance to see a large, strapping dog. It was Rage. All the canines became excited and ran to him as his owner stood behind him, unleashing him from the chain.

Dazzling exclaimed, "Oh boy!"

Everyone greeted him.

"Hi, Rage!"

"Can I get a picture with you?"

"Can I join your group?"

Following behind him was Merle, the Bedlington terrier. Her owner unleashed her and then flew to the other dog owners to brag about Merle's success at the competition.

Merle and her friends approached Dazzling. "Did you see me on TV today, Dazzling?"

Dazzling lied, "No."

Merle was far smaller than Dazzling. Her fur really did look like a sheep's.

I was baffled and said, "Aren't you Merle? We were just watch—"

Abruptly, Dazzling covered my mouth with her paw.

Merle raved, "Yes, I won the golden cup for my extraordinary talents in the pooch talent show today. Who are you?" she asked, turning to me.

I responded, "I'm Leo!" I thought *Dazzling* was showy, but that was before I met Merle.

Dazzling seized the opportunity to boast by saying, "I'm mentoring him. It's important to help young ones in the community. I'm not self-centered like *other* dogs."

One of Merle's friends, a short, small, brown and black Yorkshire terrier with pointed ears named Kia, remarked, "How noble!"

Dazzling just could not resist the urge to compete. She was showy like the others…just nicer. She sighed dramatically and said, "I am mentoring Finn also and it is not as easy as it seems to be responsible for the both of them."

"You're such a good canine, Dazzling. They are so cute! Is this their first time here?"

"Yes."

"Aww!" They made cute faces at us and patted our heads with their paws. A chocolate Labrador retriever known as Paxton asked, "So, what are your parents like?"

Baffled, I answered, "Well, my old parents owned a pet store, and my new ones always talk about some company, and Momma loves to garden."

Paxton pompously guffawed, "Are you serious? I don't mean your *owners*. What breeds were your parents? Terrier? No offense, but they're the worst. My parents are Labradors. They say that I'm the best at swimming and agility out of all my five siblings."

I wondered, *What* did *my parents look like?* I simply could not recall their appearance. I stuttered, "Uh…well, I don't remember them…I just remember living with my two sisters in the store with my Momma…I mean, my human Momma…"

A Great Dane asked, "You're adopted?"

I replied, "I was bought."

Kia chimed in, "Same difference. I have never lived in a *store*. I grew up in a litter with my parents in a house until we were of age to be adopted. Are you a designer breed, Leo?"

Designer breed. That sounded familiar.

Dazzling cut in, "He is! I believe that his owner said that he was a Maltipoo."

"Maltipoo? What kind of weird name is that?" they all replied.

I knew a few breeds from competition shows, but I did not really know the significance, and there were so many groups.

Everyone was comparing their breeds. The Great Dane snorted, "Toy breeds!"

I questioned, "What does that mean?"

He said jokingly, "You're a cross between two small breeds, so you'll be small and look like a toy forever."

Was he serious?

The Yorkshire terrier defensively retorted, "That's not all. We live inside, unlike jealous, giant, drooling, working breeds like you, Hudson. We have more jewelry. Most of us grew up with our parents and siblings and were adopted or remained at home with or without our siblings. We did not live in a cage."

Dazzling stated aloud, "Enough, guys! It doesn't matter if Leo grew up in a store or a house, with or without his birth family. Everybody is different, and things change. Remember when poodles were originally bred to be hunting dogs, and now they're companion and show dogs? Leo loves his current family."

It was kind of Dazzling to put a stop to the conversation. I was beginning to feel uncomfortable. However, I was starting to wonder about my birth parents and background. I did not remember my parents, but I had liked being with my sisters in a comfy dog bed with a tiny fence around it. In fact, I *did not see it as a cage*.

It was kind of disappointing to think that I would never grow big, strong, and tall like some dogs. Why did both of my parents have to be small?

Dazzling was surrounded by a pack of canines and even some owners, all eager to find out about me, the toy breed. Merle was swollen with envy for the attention that Dazzling was receiving.

"So, Dazzling, were you invited to Sphinx's afterparty?" she asked arrogantly. "Sphinx's owner is hosting an event to celebrate the achievements of both Sphinx and Rage in his backyard tonight. It's going to be the best party of the year."

Dazzling answered, "Oh, I don't even know. As you see, I'm *far* too busy to socialize, since I'm helping out the two little ones, who look up to me so *much*. Do you even *know* their owners?"

Merle said flatly, "No, no one can hear anything when Grands Pecky is shouting at the parrot."

The golden dog gasped and reacted sarcastically, "Why Merle, have you been living under a rock? They're Hazel and Nathan."

The other dogs gasped. "The owners of Hero?"

"Yes. I'm helping Leo to navigate his way through," responded Dazzling.

Abruptly, a coarse male voice spoke. "Did someone say the name *Hero*?"

Immediately, every dog's face became serious. All of them cowered before the assertive Rage as he haughtily approached. Even Dazzling slightly lowered her head to avoid eye contact but I did not.

One of Merle's friends answered, "Yes."

He grimaced. "I hated that dog."

Defiantly, I asked, "Why? He saved my owner's life."

Rage looked down at me with surprise at my lack of fear. He snarled, "Well, little dog, I met him when I was a puppy. He was *my* hero and I idolized him—until one day, Sphinx and I were playing with the other dogs. He humiliated me in front of everyone when I was play-fighting with Sphinx. Hero said that I could never be like him, and the other dogs laughed at me."

Dazzling then raised her head and asked in bewilderment, "What? That doesn't sound like Hero."

Rage barked, "You did not know him. He was a fraud! That weak hound didn't even like hunting!"

I yelled, "No, he's not a fraud!"

Rage roared, "Don't get so emotional, pup! You're lucky that you never even met him."

I may not have met Hero, but I could feel it in my heart that he was a good dog. Something told me that Rage was not. I growled back, and Finn placed his paw in front of me and pleaded, "Leo, he's four times our size."

The Akita wickedly chuckled, "Even a bunny has bigger brains than yours."

The other dogs laughed at us, but I did not care. I stood my ground, staring Rage down.

Suddenly, another male voice asked, "What's going on here?"

The voice was rich with sincerity, smoother, and almost princely. A cream American Akita with a black muzzle came closer, parting the pack. He wore a thick black collar with a golden tag in the shape of a pair of wings. He was just as big as Rage but a little taller and leaner, and his muzzle was longer. His face was so full of expression—not like Rage, who always looked like an angry bull ready to charge at any time.

I could see now why Dazzling preferred Sphinx. I could not believe that I had ever idolized Rage. Now I detested him for his thuggish ways. Arrogance was nothing to show off. It was just a way of bullying and making everyone fear you.

Grudgingly, Rage answered, "Nothing important, Sphinx."

Dazzling wagged her tail. "Hi, Sphinx."

"Hello, Dazzling. How are you?"

Kia announced, "She's helping to raise Leo and Finn, the new pets of Nathan and Hazel."

Sphinx stated, "Wow! That's great!"

Dazzling smirked and side-eyed Merle.

Sphinx went on, "Well, you three are welcome to join our backyard bash that our owners are having with their friends tonight. It's pup-friendly. Even the famous ferret, Fabio, is coming." The cream Akita shone a winsome smile, and all the female dogs sighed.

I thought, *Jeez, what's wrong with them?*

"Thank you," Dazzling replied casually. "I will see if I can make it with my *hectic* schedule."

Merle scoffed, while I was utterly confused about what schedule we had.

Sphinx replied, with his tongue hanging playfully out of his mouth, "Hopefully. Now, who wants to play frisbee?"

"Me! I do!" cried all the dogs.

Soon, Paisley came to us and said, "All right, guys. Time to head home."

Dazzling wanted to stay a little longer to talk to Sphinx but obeyed, and we followed her out of the park. Dazzling said to me, "Don't bother with those show-offs. Kia just watches house-designing shows all day, and Hudson is the shortest Great Dane in his family. They all have insecurities."

As we headed to the car, the ground started to vibrate, and a thunderous, roaring sound consumed the atmosphere. Finn and I shook in fear as we drew closer to Dazzling for comfort.

Finn asked, his eyes dilated, "What is *that?*"

Dazzling answered, "There's a monster truck racing track not too far from the park. Sphinx and Rage's owners usually practise there."

Paisley lamented as she looked at the tracks from afar, "Jeez, who builds a racing track so near to a park! Talk about inconsiderate people!"

Gino, who was on Grands Pecky's shoulders, started clapping and jumping in excitement. Grands Pecky asked Gino, "Do you want to see the trucks?"

Chapter 7

Leo Attends a Party

Gino smiled and nodded as he screeched, "Ouh ouh ah ah!" Grands Pecky walked to the fence of the racing compound. Paisley, who was holding Finn, called after her, "Grands! We don't have time for this!"

Grands said, "Oh, hush, child. It won't take long."

Paisley sighed, shook her head, and followed Grands to the fence. Dazzling and I stood next to her, watching the arena.

A gigantic, metallic blue monster truck sped down the tracks like a turbo-powered spaceship. I wagged my tail and panted in eagerness as the engine bellowed with power, releasing smoke like those mighty reptiles that blew fire on television.

I could not believe how enormous the truck was. The tires were huge with deep tracks, taller and bigger than me! They were like a cool, huge chew toy—every dog's dream.

Finn remarked, "Wow!"

Dazzling told us, "Sphinx's owner, Ivan, drives it. It would appear that Sphinx and Rage would have come to the park with Ivan's brother, Leroy."

The racer saw us watching and rolled his window down. He wore a helmet and waved at us, yelling enthusiastically, "Hey, Paisley! Check this!"

The truck went up a ramp and jumped midway in the air. Fiery flames then shot out from under the ramp. Wow! It was awesome! My eyes were fixated on the majestic truck, like I was caught up in a movie. I wished that I owned a truck like that.

I commented, "Whoa! That's so cool!"

Finn said, "It must have taken so much practice to make a move like that. Look at the angles!"

I was more engrossed with the spinning wheeeeels. They just went on and on in circles. Would they ever stop? I was in a trance.

Paisley and Grands Pecky's eyes grew wide with amazement, and Gino screamed with joy. The truck soon crossed the finish line, and Paisley and Grands Pecky clapped for the racer as he parked the vehicle and exited it. He was in a black and grey racing suit. He took his helmet off, revealing brown, spiky hair and a neat, slightly shaven, brown beard. He walked toward us on the other side of the fence.

"Wow! A monkey!" said the racer. "Can I pet him?"

"Go ahead, Ivan," Grands Pecky said with a smile.

Ivan pushed his fingers through the holes in the fence and touched Gino's fingers. Grands Pecky said to Ivan teasingly, "I like your truck. Maybe one day, you can take Paisley and me for a ride. It reminds me of the thrills I had when I was young and worked in the circus."

Ivan was taken aback and replied, "Okay, for sure. I would love to take Paisley and you, of course, for a ride."

Paisley quickly responded, "Hey, you two, I do not know about that."

Abruptly, Gino mischievously took Grands Pecky's hat off and placed it on his own head in his weird way of showing off to Ivan. Her blue hair was revealed, causing Paisley to cover her eyes with shame.

Ivan commented, "Gee! Awesome hair. Blue's my favorite color."

Grands smiled as she cooed, "Thanks! Gino dyed it. I'm a bit more outrageous than my workaholic granddaughter."

Ivan remarked, "Your grandma's super-cool, Paisley."

Grands boasted, "Yes, and I make beautiful granddaughters." She raised her thin grey eyebrows and winked at Paisley, who only rolled her eyes.

Ivan flashed a smile at Paisley and said, "Yes, you certainly do. By the way, I'm having a party tonight. You should swing by, so I can show you more of my stunts."

Paisley became flustered and stammered, "Oh, I don't know."

Ivan continued, "It'll be fun, I promise."

Paisley stuttered, "I…I'll see. Thanks though. Anyway, we have to go home now."

She turned around in a strangely stiff manner and almost tripped over me. Shocked, I yelped in response. *Jeez, what is going on with her,* I wondered. *Are her legs hurting?* I tilted my head as I watched her in confusion.

Paisley shrieked in surprise and embarrassment. As for her cheeks, they were a glowing red. She looked down at me and said, "Sorry, Leo!"

Ivan smirked, and Grands Pecky asked, "What's happening to you, child?"

Nervously, Paisley said, "I just lost my balance." She cleared her throat. When Ivan called out "Bye!" Paisley barely muttered "Bye" back.

I asked Dazzling, "Why is she acting like that? Does she have fleas?"

Dazzling snorted, "More like the love bug."

Still puzzled, I suggested, "She should try my flea and tick tablets. Just an ant crawling in my fur is enough to upset me."

Dazzling shook her head and laughed. "She's in *love*. Not so great at being smooth, though. Unlike me."

Finn commented in a snarky tone, "Sure."

As we got in the car, Grands Pecky offered to watch us so Paisley could attend the party. Paisley responded, "No! You can't control Gino, and I have to watch the pets and make soup."

Grands suggested, "I could make the soup, and you could go."

Paisley remarked, "I'll take up your offer on the soup, but I still don't think that I can leave you alone with all the animals."

Grands Pecky suggested, "Why don't we call that bodyguard young man from down the street. What's his name? Joe. He can help me watch the little angels for an hour or two while you take a break. I know that you made a promise to our neighbors, but darling, you are young, and you need to get out more often. I won't always be here to keep things lively for you."

Paisley sighed, "His name is Troy, and he seems nice, but—"

Grands Pecky added, "Ivan likes you."

Paisley's cheeks turned red again. Jeez, was she part tomato? She scoffed in response to hide her shyness. "Please! Ivan and his brother are just irresponsible partygoers. They are rich, so they can afford to be that way. I don't have that luxury. We are too different."

Grands insisted, "I partied a lot when I was your age. Go have fun. Do you want to be a boring old lady so early?"

Annoyed, Paisley said, "Fine! I'll go for an hour." She called Troy, Rocky's owner, and arranged for us to be looked after.

Dazzling howled, "We have to go!"

Finn reminded her, "I thought you said you were too busy."

She explained, "That's what you have to say to sound important. If we went, you two could show off your talents and your owners would enroll you in training for sure."

I said, "We don't need to go to the party. We could just stick to the plan."

The golden pooch stated, "This way is faster. Don't you want to be famous?"

I thought, *Who cares about parties? Finn and I have been fine by ourselves so far.* I answered, "Not really. I just want to make my owners proud. I don't like Rage! He insulted Hero!" The last thing

I wanted to do was make Rage feel like he was important. I did not want anything to do with him or his friends.

"It's also Sphinx's party!" Dazzling stressed. "We can stay for an hour—I have an idea."

Finn sighed. I am sure he was probably asking himself how a small bunny like him got involved with so many crazy dogs.

Later, Troy arrived with Rocky. Paisley thanked him profusely and left. Dazzling hid Rocky in the backyard so that Troy and Grands Pecky would search for him. Then Rocky ran off with us to the party.

Fanny squawked, "Rocky left the backyard!"

Troy and Grands Pecky immediately ran through the gate and chased us down the street. Grands Pecky was quite brisk for her age after running and dancing with monkeys all of her life as a circus performer.

"Rocky! Come back!" called Troy.

"Dazzling! What are you all doing?" Grands Pecky shouted. She ran beside Troy as the four of us sped away, with Finn on Dazzling's back cleverly leading us to Sphinx's extravagant house.

As we dashed through the entrance, Grands Pecky heaved a hearty sigh from chasing us and stammered, "Wh—what?"

Ivan came toward the two tired owners, greeting them. "Welcome! My brother Leroy is inside serving the food."

Grands Pecky was sweating abundantly. She stuttered, "Oh, I—I just came to get—"

Troy said in exhaustion, "It's unlike Rocky to want to go anywhere. He's always tired."

Paisley heard their voices and called out, "Grands! What are you doing here?"

Troy stated, "The pets escaped."

Paisley became frantic, but Ivan assured her, "Don't worry. They're safe in the backyard. Come inside, and I'll send someone to look for them. You guys look like you could use a soda."

Dazzling peeped out from the backyard to see what was going on and laughed in a snarky tone. Then, a familiar voice called out, "Hey, guys!"

The golden dog jumped in surprise and blurted out, "Sphinx!"

He exclaimed, "You made it!"

Nervously, Dazzling replied, "Ha ha. Fortunately, we were able to finish everything on our schedule in time. We went to the spa and the groomers. Doesn't my tail look fluffy and soft?"

The Akita laughed lightly. "It's very pretty."

"Heh heh, thank you."

Dazzling knew by now that everyone was aware that Momma was in the process of getting the rule changed, which meant that I actually stood a good chance of getting to participate in competitions. She started off, "I am training Leo and Finn for competitions. You should see them at dancing and agility."

Interested, the male dog said, "Sure!" He announced, "Everyone. Set up the agility course."

With that, dogs started setting up the backyard with the agility equipment that they used to practice. Finn nervously whispered to Dazzling, "This is a course for big dogs."

Dazzling said the same thing to Sphinx, but he disregarded her comment, saying, "Oh, we'll cheer him on either way. Right, guys?"

The dogs barked positively.

Rage commanded, "Turn on the night lights."

A dog turned them on to reveal a fluorescent-themed backyard.

I encouraged, "You can do it, Finn!"

Finn whined, "I don't know."

Dazzling pushed him to the beginning of the course. The dogs called out, "Go!"

The bunny approached the high hurdle and hopped over it, earning a happy howl from the dogs. Then, he lost his balance on the seesaw and somehow, it sent him flying into the air.

"Finn!" I yelled in fear as I instinctively dashed in his direction. Finn fell safely on my back. He was quite heavy.

The dogs cheered, "Speed, wow!"

Dazzling sighed in relief.

Amazed, Sphinx said, "Wow! Yeah! That was awesome! You are so agile, you could totally be my protégé."

Unknown to us, someone at the window had taken a video of Finn's dangerous moment.

Then Merle appeared from the pack and jeered, "Oh, please, they are good, but they need an *actual* mentor."

Dazzling growled, "Can someone turn the music up?"

A Pointer dog pressed a button on the radio. I freestyled, spun, and flipped. Then Finn hopped over me, triggering more hurrahs. I even limboed, making the dogs yelp, "Whoa! Check out little Leo!" Everyone knew that I had learnt those groovy moves from Calypso.

Ivan came to the back, along with a news reporter and film crew. They wanted to get a photo of Ivan in the truck for the cover of *Racers' Weekly*. They were all stunned by my dance performance with Finn.

Ivan called everyone else, "Guys! Check out what Nathan and Hazel's pets can do."

People snapped pictures and took videos with their cellphones; those videos went viral. The animals and people cheered loudly.

Dazzling shouted joyfully, "Good job!"

Sphinx told me, "We should hang out more, Leo. You're welcome to visit anytime you like."

Someone then pulled up with Ivan's truck. Ivan stood at the side of his truck, then said, "Hold on! I want my dog in the photo with me and my truck. My truck and Sphinx are my most prized possessions. He's a champion too, and I'm very proud of him. Come here, boy!"

Sphinx looked at me and suggested, "Hey, come join me. I'm not the only champ here."

"Really?" I asked, uncertain.

The Akita insisted, "Yeah!"

I ran with elation and quickly posed with the pair. Ivan finally sat in the driver's seat, and Sphinx and I stood below by the front tire of the truck as the reporter and film crew snapped a close photo of us. Everyone screamed in praise. Sphinx let out a big, happy bark, and I howled merrily.

I could feel Rage's sharp stare from afar. He lowly growled in jealousy with a look like I was dead meat to him. He did not seem to want anyone to be close to his brother but himself. As for my unexpected stardom, this too did not seem to sit well with him.

Abruptly, Ivan yelled, "Okay, let's ride! Hey, Paisley, hop in!"

Excited for action, the crowd pushed Paisley into the truck in the front seat next to Ivan.

So much was happening at once. Paisley cried, "I don't think I'm up for this! I don't like fast driving."

"Don't worry. I'm a pro," said Ivan reassuringly.

Grands Pecky and Finn got separated from us, and quickly, Sphinx had me up in the tray of the truck ready for a ride.

Frantically, Dazzling screamed, "Wait! Leo's a puppy!" Immediately, she ran and hopped into the tray to get me, but Ivan had started the engine, and someone closed the tray.

Dazzling yelped, "Oh no!"

Sphinx told us, "Hang on tight!"

The truck roared like a thousand lions, mighty enough to deafen us. It was like it was alive. My heart pounded eagerly. I could not believe that I was in the amazing truck. All of my dreams were coming true in just one night. Dazzling clutched tightly to me with her paw on one side and Sphinx on the opposite side.

Grands Pecky held Finn as they witnessed the scene, and Finn said, "Oh boy!"

Ivan madly drove off, past the trees, and sped off a large rock over a small pond. I shouted, "Whooaa!"

Dazzling cried in fear, "Close your eyes, Leo!"

With the speed and the jerk, Dazzling and I flew out of the tray. Dazzling landed safely on a large tuft of grass, and I fell on her tail. She howled, "Yowww! My perfectly groomed tail!"

I said, "Sorry. By the way, Dazzling, when did you get three tails?" My vision was off. I got up, feeling dizzy, and everything was spinning like the inside of the metal washing cube at home.

Immediately, Dazzling started to lick my face to help me recover. Then, with relief, she sighed, "Phew. Still intact!"

The pack of dogs roared in awe, and we greeted them on the other side. I yelled in a cracked voice, as I shook my body to regain composure, "That was fun! Let's do it again!" My fur stood up like a mohawk.

Finally, Paisley came out of the truck. Her hair looked as if she had been in a tornado. She wobbled over and awkwardly said, "Time to go."

Ivan begged, "Paisley, stay a little longer."

Firmly, she snapped, "No thanks! I've had enough. We're just too different, Ivan."

Grands Pecky firmly scolded, "Come on, Paisley. Don't be like that."

The other dogs moaned, "Aww."

Sphinx bid me goodbye with, "Nice having you."

Rage maliciously added, "You're no Hero, Leo, you ball of fluff."

His gang began to snicker, and Merle mocked, "Bye, Dazzling. Too bad your owner's a stick in the mud."

In response, Dazzling snarled.

I barked at Rage, "I want to be like Hero one day. Never like you."

Rage scowled.

Then Paisley dragged us away by our collars, and Grands Pecky quietly followed with Finn in her arm. Paisley raised her voice in fury, "What is wrong with you, Dazzling? You know that you're not allowed to leave the yard. You're not a good role model for Leo and Finn."

Dazzling whimpered and looked down, embarrassed.

Chapter 8

Leo Meets Hero

We went to bed as soon as we reached home. Grands Pecky was knocked out on the couch with the television blasting at full volume.

"From now on, you will be in your crate when I'm not home!" Paisley scolded.

Dazzling whined, "I'm sorry, boys. I wanted us to get our deserved recognition, but instead you'll be remembered as babies who got dragged away from the biggest party ever."

We sadly closed our eyes. As I fell asleep, I heard a voice calling my name…an unfamiliar male voice. It was serious yet caring…then, I saw everyone laughing at us.

The next morning, we had a quiet breakfast. Dazzling went inside her crate in the living room. She said, "Bye, guys. It was fun to have you. You two really are my boys and I love you"

I whimpered, "We love you too."

Finn melancholically said, "You have been a gracious host. Take care!"

We finally went home, and Momma greeted us by the gate. I licked all over her face. Paisley gave her the soup and Momma thanked her.

With that, a beep came from Momma's phone in her hand. It was the video of us dancing and Finn being catapulted into the air. Shocked and baffled, she asked, "What is this? Did you take Leo and Finn to some rugged monster truck party?"

Paisley nervously stammered, "My grands—she kept bugging me to go for an hour, so I got Troy to help her watch them, and they escaped and ran to the party. Please, Hazel, you know that I'm not like that."

"They could have gotten hurt by those bigger dogs, Paisley."

"I know, and I'm sorry."

Warily, Momma said, "I need time to process this. Nathan will be angry."

Paisley sighed and left. I whined sadly. I felt sad for Paisley and Dazzling. Momma was mad at Paisley, and Paisley was mad at Dazzling for trying to help us. Come to think of it, I felt sorry even for Grands Pecky, who chased after us. It was not nice of us to make her run so far and become exhausted at her age. I had not even realized that until now.

We went inside to see Papa, who was on the recliner with his feet slightly raised up. "Hey, boys! I missed you so much."

Momma lifted each of us to greet Papa by his face. Momma told Papa everything, and he became immensely upset, but she tried to calm him down. With that, Momma gave him a glass of water and a laptop and left for a meeting.

Finn and I went outside so that I could check on the plants. We went into the doghouse to make more growth mixture.

Finn called out, "Straw, fur..."

I yawned, "I had a weird dream that everyone laughed at us."

Finn said, "Post trauma."

I added, "There was a voice…no idea who it was."

Finn said, "Hmph. Not sure what that means."

I joked, "Are you a vet?"

I added more things to a big bowl and mixed everything up with my paw.

"Pieces of discarded lemon, dried leaves, scraps of vegetables, and…a clover leaf."

Surprised, Finn asked, "Where did you get that?"

I said, "Found it in the park."

Finn was genuinely confused and stated, "There are no clover trees in the park."

"It was just on the grass." As I mixed everything up, it gave off a bad smell. I yelped, "Whoa!" The smell filled the doghouse.

Suddenly the entire doghouse shook with power. I shrieked, "What's happening?"

Finn whimpered, "I don't know!"

I howled and immediately, everything ceased shaking. I asked, "Was that an earthquake?"

Abruptly, a resonant bark erupted from outside of the doghouse. Finn wondered in panic, "Is someone outside? It could be Rage seeking revenge."

I stuttered, "I—I'll check it out."

"Be careful!" Finn called behind me.

I slowly stepped outside of the doghouse with caution, yelling, "Who's there! I'm not afraid!" The bark did not sound like Rage's or Sphinx's. I tried not to cower.

Suddenly, a figure appeared in front of me. An American foxhound dog stood before my eyes, wearing a leather collar with a pendant of two swords clashing. Finn came out to see what was happening, and we gasped.

Finn confusedly questioned, "Is it—?"

The dog spoke. "I'm Hero."

We looked at each other in bewilderment and fear. I mumbled, "Aren't you…not alive?"

The towering dog looked down at me with his gentle, brown eyes and answered in a sophisticated voice, "I'm here because you summoned me."

I asked, "I did?"

Hero explained, "The clover leaf was there for you. Long ago, new dogs would be led by the souls of previous dogs who lived with their families. It's rarer now because dogs began to adapt to their new families more quickly. You have been gifted with exceptional capabilities that I must help you to harness. I, your soul guide, am here to help you to find your true potential."

Finn asked, "Is he the only dog in the neighborhood with a soul guide?"

Hero answered, "Well, Leo is one of the few canines in generations. Only a few dogs are deemed worthy of having a soul guide now. Some humans have them too, and they're called guardian angels."

Finn said, "Wow."

I asked, "Can you help me get my lucky charm?"

He said, "You have already discovered your talent."

"What is it?"

"Luck. It means that you have been granted success in anything you do, as long as you make an effort," Hero explained.

My jaw dropped. "Anything?"

"Yes. You will see your lucky charm very soon."

"Awesome!" I exclaimed. "Hero…did you really save my Momma from a bear attack?"

His face became serious as he answered, "I did, and I would do it again."

Sadly, I said, "They really missed you."

He sighed, "I know they found Finn and you."

I asked, "Do you miss them?"

"I do."

"Are we the only ones who can see you?"

"Yes," said Hero. "Maybe a few of your closest friends might be able to see me."

I asked one last question: "Why does Rage hate you?"

Hero sighed and sat as he began, "When Rage was a pup, I saw him playing with his friends, and his rage overtook him. I could see the fury in his eyes even then. He wanted to hurt his brother to show off his power to the others. I stopped him in front of everyone. They laughed at him, but I had to step in. He was too violent for a puppy. I told him that I was not trying to humiliate him, but he was too proud and stubborn to see my correction in any other way. That happens sometimes, when puppies aren't socialized well enough with their mothers. They don't know the limits and can't accept discipline for the consequences of their actions."

He paused in grave reflection and continued, "After that, Rage held a grudge and always tried to embarrass me. But one day, he took it too far."

"How?"

"One day, he tried to attack me while no one was around at home, but I restrained him again and let him go. Since then…" He sadly looked away.

"Wow."

Hero warned, "That is why you must *listen* to me. Rage is an evil dog. You must stay as far from him as possible. You don't know what he is capable of."

Finn wailed, "Too late! We've already upset him by stealing his spotlight."

"That means he'll be planning to get you two soon," warned Hero.

I asked, "What about Sphinx?"

"He's not bad," said Hero.

Finn inquired, "Should we ask Sphinx to tell Rage to leave us alone?"

Hero said, almost ominously, "Rage listens to no one. It would mean a battle between brothers."

I said, "Oh no! Rage could be after Dazzling too! We can't let him hurt her!"

Finn explained who Dazzling was. The taller dog assured us, "Don't worry. You all will be safe for now—until your talent becomes undeniable." He continued, "For now, let's just do things as you usually do."

Soon, we saw Momma's light blue car heading to the house. She greeted us in the yard but was not able to see Hero. However, she looked around strangely as though she felt his presence. Then, she shrugged off the feeling and glanced at her plants.

"Hmph! The honeysuckle actually has young buds. This is the first time that this plant has shown any signs of blossoming. The violets look dry. I watered them before I went to work yesterday," she commented.

She rushed inside to change to attend to her garden. I rushed into the red doghouse and returned with a plastic bottle of water, which was riddled with holes pierced by my teeth. I passed the bottle over the violets, to give them a gentle shower. Then I gently pushed the potted plant away from the sunlight.

Chapter 9

Leo Gets His Lucky Charm

Momma came back and saw me. "Leo?"

I turned toward her in response, with the half-empty bottle of water in my jaw.

Finn whimpered, "Oh boy."

Momma ran toward me and asked in disbelief, "Have you been watering my plants?"

I whined.

She lifted me up, saying, "Thank you! Thank you! Good dog! You're brilliant!" I loved being lifted up. I tried to lick her face but she would not let me. Momma then sped inside with me and told Papa.

Papa joked, "Well, he must have known that you were doing something wrong. I believe that we are pretty lucky to have such a smart dog."

"Yes, lucky. I know which pendant belongs to you now. From now on, I will buy plants, and you will decide what to do with them."

Hero somehow appeared in the house with Finn, and he smiled at me. I smiled back.

The next day, Momma bought me a dog tag in the shape of a clover leaf. She cooed, "Leo Pomp, our lucky little gardener." With that, they headed to work.

Finn exclaimed, "Congrats, Leo."

Hero then appeared. "I see that you got your charm."

"Yes! And I'm grateful, really. I just want to do more."

Hero responded, "You will. It's just not right to enter a puppy into such intense competitions. You don't want to end up like Rage."

I whined, "I'm going to be six months soon."

"Just give them some time. Nathan is still healing from his injury."

I sighed, "Okay."

Papa and Momma briefly returned for a lunch break. As they exited the car, Momma spoke aloud, "I'm telling you, Nathan. I showed pictures of our garden to my colleagues, and they said that we should enter a garden competition. Leo is our secret gardener. The flowers are good enough to be used at weddings!"

"So, why don't we sell them to wedding planners?" Papa suggested.

Momma yelped, "I don't want to sell my precious flowers when we could have a chance at winning the competition!"

"I don't know, Haze. That's a lot of pressure to place on the poor guy. We don't need publicity."

"It's not so bad," said Momma. "Hey, I do the planting, watering, and spraying to prevent plant diseases, mister! I do my share," she added confidently. "Besides, most of our neighbors began entering their dogs into competitions at his age."

"This isn't a dog competition," Papa insisted.

"The purple orchids are blooming so well, and the Osiria rose is beginning to shoot out flower buds," said Momma excitedly. "This plant is one of the rarest types of rose. It's one of my treasures." She continued, "Nate, I love flowers. My garden brings me serenity. I just want others to feel it too."

Finally, Papa said, "Fine. We can give it a try."

"Thank you, Nathan!" Momma turned to me. "We're entering the garden competition!" She gently cupped my face with her hands, and I whimpered affectionately.

Then, the two adults headed inside.

Finn said, "Sorry that you're not training for the dog competition. I know how badly you wanted it."

I sighed, "It's okay. Momma really wants to show her flowers to everyone, and we should support her. We can't only focus on what we want."

Finn responded, "That's noble of you, Leo. I agree. I'm going inside for food."

I stayed outside and enjoyed the breeze. Hero then appeared on the porch and remarked, "Spoken like a true, wise dog. It's what we do. We place our owners' needs before our own and in turn, they do the same for us. Our bond with humans relies on sacrifice in trying to understand each other. That's what real love is."

He sat next to me and stared at the garden. I observed him and realized just how genuine Hero's words were. I wondered aloud, "Were you a hunting dog?"

He answered, "Yes, but I didn't enjoy hunting like my siblings. When our family adopted me, I realized that I liked agility and frisbee. Your breed does not define you, Leo."

It was nice to know that a respected dog like Hero did not let anything decide his future. It made me feel accepted for who I was.

I started thinking about how Hero did not care about fame and power like the other dogs in the neighborhood. Dazzling was a good friend, with her heart in the right place, but she did not quite understand that lesson yet.

I remembered when I asked Hero about his pendant, he said, "It means honor. Fight for what you believe in no matter what."

I asked him, "Do you think that I have honor?"

Hero had looked down at me at that moment, chuckled lightly, and said, "Yes! You're braver than any canine I've ever met. That's why I was sent here to guide you."

Now, Finn hopped through the dog door, breathless. "Momma called about enrolment for the garden competition and she found out that the judging takes place soon."

Hero announced, "Well, we should get started." We began to sniff around the entire yard for all sorts of things that could help to grow the plants—wood ash, grass clippings—and add them to the soil of the plants.

The next week, the other plants began to sprout tiny buds. The honeysuckle vine had grown larger and taller, with more honeysuckle blooming from the buds. It was a beautiful sight to see. It was almost like magic.

Soon, Dazzling was free again from the crate, thanks to Grands Pecky taking pity on her. She slipped out of her house to visit us when Grands fell asleep. Feeling like a spy, Dazzling told us, "I have to be back before four o'clock! The latest scoop I got is that Ivan called Paisley. I think that those two like each other."

We were indifferent to this news, because our minds were elsewhere.

"By the way," she said to me, "you have been invited to the dog dancing club." To Finn, she said, "There's actually a bunny community in the neighborhood that wants you to join!"

Then she noticed my clover pendant. "You got your lucky charm! I'm guessing luck?"

I said, "Yes. Also, I have so much to tell you. I saw Hero."

Dazzling stepped back with a perplexed look.

"He came to me," I explained. "He's my soul guide." Then I asked Hero, "Can you show yourself to her?"

Hero appeared, very visible to her, causing her to gasp, "How is it possible?"

Hero explained everything to Dazzling, who replied, "Wow! I'm so proud of you, Leo!" She looked at Hero and said, "It is an honor to meet you, Hero."

He smiled. "Thank you for being a good friend to Leo and Finn."

"Well, I wasn't so great. I got us all in trouble," sighed Dazzling.

I said reassuringly, "You are. You made sure that our talents were seen. My parents may consider enrolling us in competitions soon."

"Oh, I'm so glad to hear that, Leo," said Dazzling.

Playfully, Hero suggested, "Why don't we head to the park for some fun?"

We grabbed a ball to play with and followed an owner walking her dog so that it appeared we had come with a human.

At the park, all the canines sped to us.

"You guys were amazing at Rage and Sphinx's party!"

"Can I have your pawprint?"

Dazzling announced, "We thank you, fans, but these two are taking a break right now. In fact, Finn and Leo are currently helping their owners for a garden competition. They never stop working, so do not disturb them. However, I will answer any questions you all have."

Rage then appeared and greeted me. "Sorry that you had to go home early to drink your bottle," he snarled. "And now, you're playing with flowers?"

His friends cackled loudly. A friend of Rage then snorted, "And he thinks his owners are his Mommy and Daddy!"

I rolled my eyes at their silly jabs.

No one else could see Hero, but he could see them. He commented, "Rage has grown larger in size since my final encounter with him and so has his venom."

Hero growled at Rage, but Rage could not hear him. He only felt an odd presence. Slightly alerted, Rage asked his friends, "Do you guys feel that?"

"Feel what?" they asked.

"A weird feeling like someone's watching."

Finn and I were surprised and confused. Hero informed us, "Dogs can feel the presence of spirits but not see them. The others can't feel my presence because they're not paying attention."

We approached Dazzling and signaled that it was time to leave in an attempt to get away from Rage. As Dazzling was saying goodbye to some of her friends, the rest of the dogs in the park kept raving about us.

"Leo has the freshest hairstyle."

"Finn's fur is so soft."

"Dazzling is so pretty."

Rage was aggravated and overheard Merle complaining to a friend, "Why is Dazzling getting so much attention? She hasn't performed for months. The puppy and bunny are cute, but it's so obvious that they're just being used as a hoax. And planting? What kind of skill is that! Has everyone lost their minds?"

Rage drew nearer to Merle and I overheard him coyly comment, "You're afraid of being washed away by their modern antics, aren't you?"

She retorted, "Of course not! I'm just too intelligent to fall for Dazzling's tricks."

Rage continued, "I have an idea. I can put in a good word for you with Sphinx, if you do me one favor."

Warily, she asked, "What is it?"

The burly Akita answered, "Find out when that stupid flower competition will be." At first, I thought he was just being nosey, since I had become taciturn towards him. However, I was wrong.

Chapter 10

Leo Discovers the Truth

M omma had supplied us with more soil and water. She did a
fairly good job planting; I did the rest, nurturing and adding
nourishment.

I added a compost heap of manure, old leaves, weeds, and even
leftover pieces of bread. I already had the honeysuckles blooming
a bright pink, with yellow and a little white. They looked fluffy
and colorful at the entrance gate, which led the way to the blue and
purple bellflowers.

Momma exclaimed, "Oh my! Everything looks fabulous, Leo!
We'll win for sure! I am so happy and excited for the judges to see
to the signature piece of this garden, our Osiria rose. Everyone
was so amazed that I was able to get it to actually bloom and be so
bright, since this type of rose was known to have poor plant health! I
could not do all of this without your help, Leo. You are such a good
gardener!" Then, she left to buy more humus.

The week before the competition, everything was almost set, and we
were all filled with eagerness. I had just turned six months old and
was feeling proud that I had grown.

Then, out of nowhere, five dogs appeared by our gate: Malik, Wayne, Ted, and some strange dog. They were led by Rage. He leaped over the fence, and the others followed.

Instantly, I knew that Merle must have told Rage the date of the competition. Still, I questioned, "What are you doing here?"

Wickedly, Rage hissed, "Just joining the party." With that, he yanked a bunch of bluebells out of the grass and ripped them apart.

I yelled, "What are you doing!"

The other dogs began to dig holes in the garden, damaging the flower beds. They clawed at the nasturtium shrubs with their paws and crushed the sunflowers.

Enraged, I shouted, "Stop it!"

They were not listening and kept wreaking chaos in Momma's garden.

I dashed toward Wayne and bit his leg. He snarled, "Quit it before I take a bite out of you!"

Finn frantically tried to collect some of the uprooted bellflowers and store them in the doghouse.

I barked, "This is my home! I won't let you destroy it!"

Rage chuckled, "Such spirit."

I growled at him, and he growled back.

Hero then appeared and warned, "Be careful, Leo! Don't try to fight him."

I wanted to ignore him, but I screamed, "He's ruining my hard work."

Hero revealed, "He can kill you like he killed me!"

My eyes widened and my jaw fell as I whispered in disbelief. "What?"

Hero explained, "He lured the bear to the hiking site so that I would rescue our mother. He was hiding behind the trees where the bear had come from."

Rage was a murderer? My realization of Hero's words about Rage and his taking his hatred too far had deepened. As my thoughts sank in, I felt hot tears well up in my eyes, but I fought them back.

Cherisse Sudan

As Rage started to approach Momma's prized Osiria rose, I spat, through gritted teeth, seething with anger, "You killed Hero!"

Rage stopped in his tracks. He quickly turned away from the rose plant and faced me. He attempted to conceal his shock and said, "Don't be ridiculous, wimp!"

I growled louder than I had ever growled before. "You're a killer! You were jealous of Hero! You led the bear to him!"

The other dogs watched me like I was not right in the head, and they watched Rage to see his reaction.

Rage screeched, "Shut your mouth, rat. Stop talking nonsense before I make you!"

I growled at him in a face-off. We saw the furious hatred in each other's eyes. I barked ferociously and incessantly, "I am not scared of you! I will stand for my family forever!" I did not care what Rage would do to me anymore.

Abruptly, Finn disappeared and returned with a jar of ants. There were tiny holes on the lid. Angrily, Finn kicked the jar open with his hind legs in the direction of the dogs. The ants quickly scattered onto the dogs.

The ants bit their bodies, injecting their venom, causing them to howl in pain. Soon, their entire bodies were covered with the insects. They had bumps on every inch of their skin as they continuously scratched with their claws.

Still, Rage held his ground. He did not flinch or whimper. He only growled, "Do you think that stupid ants could scare me off? I'm not a loser like you and your friend. I told you not to mess with me. You are nothing, and Hero was nothing!"

The fuming Akita barked and abruptly lunged toward me. Instantly, Hero stepped in front of me, and Rage could see him.

Hero demanded, "Stop, Rage!"

Rage's face became blank and haunted. He stepped back and crouched down.

Malik and the others could not see Hero and became confused as to what was happening.

Rage stuttered in shock, "No…how…it's not you—"

Hero gazed menacingly at him with intense disapproval and anger. He growled, "You took me from my family. You are a disgrace to yours. Leo is the dog of luck. I am protecting him. Leave or you will spend an eternity seeing my face."

Rage's eyes were filled with fear, for the first time. Then, Hero barked in front of his face and Rage shouted in fright, "No! I'm sorry about the bear! Please! You need to know that I did not mean for it to happen like that!" The other dogs could not understand who Rage was speaking to, as he kept repeating, "I did not want that to happen to you!" They all thought that Rage was insane or delirious.

Then, Dazzling and Sphinx came running towards the yard with a small pack of other dogs and Finn, who had apparently escaped to find them. Dazzling gasped at the sight, "Oh my goodness! Leo, are you okay? Stay away from him, Rage!"

Angrily, Sphinx shouted, "Rage! How could you do this?"

Wayne whined, "He's losing it! He's seeing Hero!"

Dazzling and the small pack of dogs gasped in horror and Hero became invisible again. Rage quickly came to his senses, shook his head, and stood straight again. His face was solemn, and he was silent.

Disbelief plagued their faces. Ashamed, Sphinx barked, "You need to leave now, Rage."

Rage stood upright once more, regained his composure, and glared at me with eyes filled with mixed emotions. As the confused Akita silently began to walk out of the yard, Rage turned around and viciously tore one of the hanging honeysuckle plants apart with his fangs, chewed it, and spat it out. The other dogs all scowled at him and gasped. Even at his most shameful moment, he was still arrogant and filled with malice. He then left, followed by his itching friends.

Filled with guilt, Sphinx announced to his friends, "Let's help Leo fix what my brother has ruined." They all tried to assist by filling the holes back up, putting the flowers back in the soil and some into pots. They tried to rake with their paws the messy, shaken leaves and petals. But the garden no longer looked as ravishing and tidy as before.

Cherisse Sudan

I went back into the doghouse and asked Hero what to do. He answered, "You have found your true potential. Nature trusts you. Recollect what you did the first time you learned to grow plants."

I thought about what he said and it hit me. Quickly, I instructed everyone, "Bring all the discarded food stuff from the bins that you can find."

Immediately, the dogs obeyed and scampered out of the yard.

Just then, my parents arrived home, appalled at the scene. My momma cried, "What happened to my garden, Leo?" She looked at me with a hurt and disappointed expression on her face.

Oh no! I tried to wag my tail against Momma, but she moved away from me. A few seconds later, Momma grabbed my collar, attached a long leash, and left me in the doghouse. I tugged to get free, yelling loudly at first, and then I was reduced to a tired whimper, "No! I am a good dog! I am a good dog! I do good-dog things. I promise!" My heart ached, but Momma didn't respond.

I spent that night chained in the doghouse, with my head on my paws, dejected about the situation. Tears filled my eyes. It was a night empty of warmth and love, and I sulked through it all in despair. I hated being away from everybody, isolated and alone, looking from the outside like the outcast of the family—the villain. It was torturous, like being in a prison.

It was only then that I realized the painful difference between my momma, papa, and me. No matter what I said, they could not hear my words, despite our love for one another. That was what all of the dogs had been telling me all along. That was why the dogs laughed at me for calling them my parents. We spoke in different ways and were from different worlds. But they *were* my parents to me, although they could not understand me. They always would be.

I felt so defeated and hopeless. I just wanted to help my momma, the one I loved so much. That was all I have ever wanted—to make her smile and be proud of me. I was crushed.

Chapter 11

Leo is a Hero

Now, Momma saw me as something that I did not want to be: a disappointment, a bad dog. My spirit was broken, my heart was heavy with sadness. The night was long and painful. My eyes were tired from crying. I missed my parents. It was like I had not seen them in ages.

What more could I do? I knew in my heart that I was a good dog. I could hear Hero telling me in my mind, "Don't give up, Leo. You must keep trying. Keep believing." How much longer could I?

I had done everything that was possible, and things were still ruined. I closed my fatigued eyes that were red from howling and crying. I had to hope with every fiber of my being that somehow, I could save the garden.

The next morning, Papa went to work, and Momma decided to stay home to clean up the garden. It was Paisley's arrival that prompted speech to return to my mother's mouth. Momma explained what she thought happened. Fortunately for me, Paisley said, "It might not have been Leo. The neighbor said that she saw a bunch of dogs fighting in your yard yesterday."

Momma exclaimed, "Fighting!" Immediately, she ran to Finn and me to see if we were hurt.

Momma cried, "Oh, Leo Pomp! I'm so sorry for chaining you up last night! It hurt my heart so much last night to hear you howl!" I licked her hands generously to show that I forgave her and whined lovingly. Her words meant the world to me. She believed me at last. I felt like I was home again, no longer cast away on a ship like those people on the television, sailing farther and farther away from their families on land, breaking their connections and bonds.

Abruptly, Rage's owner, Leroy, came to the gate, fuming. He raised his voice as he called out, "Hazel, did you poison my dog?"

Both Paisley and Momma asked in a shocked tone, "What?"

Leroy stated angrily, "I know that there was some dog fight here. Did you try to kill my dog?"

Paisley quickly defended Momma. "How dare you accuse my friend of something so cruel! She wouldn't do such a thing! Your dog is vicious by nature! All of the other dogs on the street are scared of him."

Leroy responded sharply, "There it is, and that's why she tried to poison him. But the vet is on her way."

Paisley snapped, "What was Rage doing unleashed and unaccompanied by a dog walker in Miss Hazel's yard anyway?"

I became intensely annoyed. How could he say that about my poor momma? She was the sweetest, gentlest person in the world.

I started to growl lowly at him and protectively stood in front of my momma.

Startled, Momma watched me and said, "Leo! Don't growl." I obeyed reluctantly.

Frustrated, Leroy continued, "All I know is that my dog is really sick now after being in your yard."

Paisley asked, "Well, how come the other dogs aren't ill like Rage?"

Leroy declared, "I know why! She singled him out!"

Momma stammered, "No! I didn't even know about the fight."

Paisley rebutted for Momma. "Those dogs shouldn't even have been in her yard. Her home isn't a fighting arena."

Suddenly, it hit me. Rage had bitten the honeysuckle. It must have caused Rage to get sick.

Instinctively, I sped to the battered vines of flowers and carefully nudged the tattered honeysuckle petals with my nose, toward Momma. She came closer and bent down, examining it, and her eyes grew wide.

Momma blurted out, "He must have chewed the honeysuckle flowers! Some believe it to be non-poisonous, but it can cause an allergic reaction. Therefore, it mostly likely contains some sort of toxin. What if this makes it poisonous to dogs? Leo doesn't chew plants and flowers. That's why nothing happens to him."

Paisley and Leroy were surprised. Then Paisley retorted at Leroy, "Well, you need to alert the vet immediately of this. But you apologize to Hazel for accusing her of poisoning your violent dog."

Leroy stuttered, "Okay, okay, I'm sorry." Immediately, he left, yelling, "I am going to let the vet know now."

I thought, *How strange. The same thing that Rage mocked me for ended up getting him sick.* I was frightened for him.

Paisley shook her head in annoyance, commenting, "Like owner, like pet. His brother is so much more charming."

Momma smiled at her and said, "Thanks for defending me, but I feel so badly."

Paisley shrugged. "You didn't know that the plant could be harmful to dogs. Plus, you didn't intend for the dog to be harmed. Poor guy must be worried about his dog though."

Momma sighed and stared at the honeysuckle, finally saying, "When I bought this house, this plant was always here. It just was not vining yet. I have researched other plants that I planted to make the yard a pet-friendly environment, but I never really checked on the honeysuckle. I hope that Rage is okay."

"Me too. Anyway, what are you going to do now?" Paisley asked.

Momma gathered her thoughts and sighed, "Nathan said that I'd probably have to withdraw from the competition."

Paisley suggested, "Do you need help?"

Momma shook her head and answered, "No, you have helped a lot already, and I only have a week left. It's not enough time."

Paisley nodded sadly.

I had no clue how to tell Momma that I was trying to fix this. All I could do was lick her.

The next day, Momma signed the withdrawal papers and went with me to deposit them into the neighbor's mailbox, which was a few houses away. The moment Momma went back inside our home, I was back up the road trying to get the withdrawal papers out of the mailbox. She may have given up, but that was not my plan.

Luckily for me, I saw Pixie basking in the early morning sun. She was a lovely calico cat and, as my friend, she inquired, "Leo, what are you trying to do?"

I explained everything, and quickly, Pixie sprang up onto the mailbox and pawed at the door with her sharp claws. In no time, she alighted from the mailbox with the forms in her mouth and gave them to me.

Later, all of the dogs had a meeting in Sphinx's yard to get an update on Rage's condition.

Sphinx said, "Rage is going to be all right. Although he chewed the honeysuckle, he spat it out, so he was not badly affected."

Dazzling said, "We are so happy to hear that he'll be okay."

Sphinx explained, "Rage's contact with the honeysuckles had him delirious and thinking that he had seen Hero."

Dazzling looked at me, and I signaled to her not to say anything by slightly shaking my head. I said, "Yes, he did claw at the honeysuckles. Sphinx, I am sorry for all that happened."

Sphinx answered, "It was not your fault. Rage does not deserve to get ill, but he started everything."

Dazzling said, "Well, tell Rage that we wish him a speedy recovery. We will see you later." We left, and so did the other dogs.

The other dogs came in front of my gate and asked what my mother was going to do now that the garden was not fit for a competition. I explained everything and brought the forms out to show them. Hudson, the Great Dane, asked, "What are we going to do with them?"

Kia, the Yorkshire terrier, exclaimed, "Eat them, obviously, Hudson."

A Dalmatian, called Domino, said, "But I'm not allowed to eat homework anymore."

I announced, "Everyone! We need to get rid of the evidence."

Dazzling explained, "If we tear it up, Leo's owner can still compete."

I ordered, "We need to get rid of the evidence. It has to be a team effort."

With that, the dogs said collectively, "Okay!" and "Sure!" Then, they surrounded the pages on the grass in a circle and made a pledge: "As code of the canines, we pledge to tear these sheets of paper to help Leo and his owner with the garden competition. We will rip and eat the pages in the spirit of friendship. May the first wolf and the first hound grant us success."

All the dogs howled as a unit. Kia chewed and swallowed a large piece and remarked, "Gee! It's so warm and tastes good."

Domino started to scratch his neck and yelped, "I think I'm allergic. Must be counteracting my allergy meds." He was always complaining about his sensitive skin.

Hudson rolled his eyes as he chewed and mumbled, "It's all in your head, Domino."

Dazzling whispered between chews, "It tastes blander than chow."

I laughed. I loved to rip paper apart. It was fun and even more enjoyable with all of the other dogs around. Everybody seemed so much closer to each other and less divided than before. Finn, as usual, was part of everything. He loved shredding paper too. His teeth worked like a shredding machine.

As the days went by, the dogs would bring all sorts of things they found in their yards. The plastic bottles and soda cans, I sent back. I kept the used tea bags, banana peels, and eggshells from breakfast; they were the best.

A French bulldog called Chopper brought a half-eaten sandwich, but by the time I was ready for it, he had gulped it down.

All the crazy things that everyone brought were useful to the plants.

Domino said, "Don't worry, guys. I'll take care of watering the plants. My house has a big tank of water." Every day, he would dip his drinking bowl into his owners' aquarium and bring it to us. Boy, did it smell fishy, but delicious. Of course, the yard did not look clean, but we were doing what was necessary to revive the plants first.

One morning, Paisley was walking Dazzling and gasped "Oh my!" with delight. They stopped, and Paisley immediately rang our doorbell. "How are you, Haze?" she asked when Momma opened the door.

Momma responded, "I'm all right. Still trying to get over this. I had such hope that we could win."

"What are you talking about?" Paisley asked. "You know, the yard doesn't look super-bad. Your Osiria rose is still growing so beautifully. The bellflowers and impatiens are all looking healthy.

Besides, no one's yard is looking good these days. Everyone in the neighborhood has their trash all over the place."

Confused, Momma asked, "What?"

Paisley explained, "Neighbors have been complaining about it. Even me! My trash can has been knocked over with trash everywhere every day, and I don't know why. Everybody initially thought that it was raccoons, but Rocky's owner found him with an empty plastic bottle, and Ivan admitted that Sphinx has been acting weirdly. Maybe it's the dogs?"

Nervously, Dazzling whined and looked down, knowing that we were involved. Momma noticed and glanced at me suspiciously. I groaned lightly, resting my head on my paws. She probably realized that I was up to something, given that she had seen the banana peels in the soil as well.

Then Paisley commented again with excitement, "As I was saying, Haze, your plants still look so strong and big. Hey—you wouldn't mind if I snapped a photo of your rose, right?"

Perplexed as to what was being said, Momma quickly made her way to the garden. She eyed the flowers with uncertainty and touched them to try to convince herself that what she was seeing was real.

Over the next few days, Momma recognized rapid growth recoveries, especially in the lilies, orchids, and honeysuckle vines. She realized that Paisley was right.

"Nate! Look! The plants have revived and grown even stronger! The flowers look bigger, brighter, and actually, the plants themselves are thicker too! Just look at the stalks, and…oh my, my Osiria rose has truly grown! It used to take so long and now, it's all full! I—I can't believe it! It's a miracle!"

Papa responded, "Wow. How did they all revive so quickly after all the trauma?"

She smiled at me. "Leo Pomp! I knew that you were up to something like always. Wait, this means that I can re-enter the competition…but I already signed the withdrawal papers. I need to call them." She called, but no one was answering. She announced, "I have to go to the competition center headquarters."

Immediately, she got dressed and hopped into her car. Papa wished her good luck and she sped away. Then, he headed off to a meeting.

Momma was on a mission. She headed for the headquarters with renewed sense of purpose and hope. Once home, she explained, "I hustled breathlessly to the headquarters and was told that there was no record of a withdrawal letter from me. The receptionist said the judges are coming in three days to inspect my garden. Nate, I am still in the competition."

Momma broke into a smile. She could not believe how fortunate she was to have everything back in order after such a devastating mess. Papa, Finn, and I were delighted to see her happy once more. Finn sighed, "Phew." After that, we spent a lot of time cleaning up the garden.

The day before the judges came, Momma bought new, brightly colored pots to replace the ones that were broken. Dazzling and I thanked the dogs. Surprisingly, they were all eager to see the competition. That night, everyone at my home fell asleep early.

The next morning, we awoke very early, filled with anticipation. The judges were already outside. Even Sphinx's friends pulled their owners toward our house while on their walks.

Hero smiled at me and winked, saying, "Go get 'em, winner. Thank you for taking care of our family and bringing them hope and joy. You *are* a hero."

His words warmed my heart and brought a smile across my face. I said, "Thanks for always supporting me."

Finn sat by the porch, and I ran onto the pathway. The judges saw me, and our parents glanced at me anxiously after welcoming the judges, who came with a camera crew.

A gentle breeze passed through, causing the leaves of the plants to softly sway. All the leaves moved in a beautiful yet peaceful choreography. The butterflies flew on the flowers and around the judges, who were examining Momma's precious Osiria rose, lilies, orchids, and camellia plants.

Everybody around stared in awe. One judge commented, "Osiria roses are rare to find. It's like nature timed everything perfectly." The judges, as well as neighbors, snapped pictures. Immediately, they declared Momma's garden for first place. My parents were overcome with pride and joy.

The camera zoomed in on them as the judges asked, "How did you do this?"

Momma held me, and replied, "We have our lucky puppy, Leo Pomp, and our shy bunny, Finnley. Everything Leo touches turns to gold. He gives us hope and never gives up. Leo is the world's best gardener and a great dog."

I was extremely touched by her words. This was all that I had ever wanted.

Papa added, "We plan to sign him up for dog competitions soon and our bunny, too. When you have a wonderful family, your home shows it."

I could not believe it. They were going to start training us to compete.

Finn zoomed around the garden and did several small flips, yelling, "Whoo! We did it, Leo!"

Dazzling cried happily, "I'm so proud of you guys!"

The other dogs howled, "Go Leo! Go Finn!" Then, they asked, "What's your secret to luck?"

I responded, "Well, I learned that you must believe in yourself and your dreams, no matter what others say. Also, it is important to have friends you can count on, like our wonderful mentor, Dazzling and my buddy, Finnley." I thought to myself, *And you as well, Hero. You as well.*

The End

Cherisse Sudan

Printed in the United States
by Baker & Taylor Publisher Services